THE PAWNS OF DEATH

The chess match was to continue until one of the players lost his king or gave up. No one dreamed that the game was for higher stakes than winning. Yet Charlie Chan found death to be the third player.

CHARLIE CHAN BOOKS

Charlie Chan's Words of Wisdom,
by Howard M. Berlin

BOOKS BY EARL DERR BIGGERS
(creator of Charlie Chan)

The Agony Column
Fifty Candles

BY JOHN KENDRICK BANGS

The Dreamers: A Club
Raffles Holmes & Company

BY GUY BOOTHBY

Dr. Nikola
The Lust of Hate

BY MICHAEL BRACKEN,

Deadly Campaign
Psi Cops
Tequila Sunrise
Bad Girls
All White Girls
Fedora (editor)

BY LEIGH BRACKETT

The Tiger Among Us

BY ROBERT COLBY

The Captain Must Die
Secret of the Second Door
Make Mine Vengeance

BY ERNEST DUDLEY

Alibi and Dr. Morelle

BY DAVID DVORKIN

The Cavaradossi Killings
Time for Sherlock Holmes

BY JOHN RUSSELL FEARN

The Tattoo Murders
Account Settled
Liquid Death and Other Stories

THE PAWNS OF DEATH

BILL PRONZINI &
JEFFRY WALLMANN

(writing as Robert Hart Davis)

WILDSIDE PRESS

THE PAWNS OF DEATH

A Charlie Chan Mystery

Originally published in *Charlie Chan Mystery Magazine*, August 1974.

Published by:
Wildside Press
P.O. Box 301
Holicong, PA 18928-0301
www.wildsidepress.com

I

CHARLIE CHAN and Prefect Claude DeBevre returned to the Hotel Frontenac from their sightseeing tour of Paris late in the afternoon. They were pleasantly tired and in high spirits, for they had visited the Eiffel Tower, Sacre Coeur, Napoleon's Tomb, Les Invalides and that compelling mosaic of great art, the Louvre.

The quaintness, the color, the contrasts, the great ambiance of Paris had touched Chan deeply; and DeBevre had enjoyed revisiting the attractions of his city as much as his guest.

The portly detective was in the French capital on a rare pleasure trip, having been one of those privileged individuals personally invited to attend the Transcontinental Chess Tournament. His interest in, and love of, the intricate game was well known throughout the chess world; and yet, typically, he was both surprised and honored to receive the invitation.

Chan had not had a vacation in some time, and since he was not involved in a case, he was delighted to accept.

Through Prefect DeBevre, whom he had met during a crime conference in San Francisco, he had made reservations weeks earlier at the Frontenac—he was, in fact, quartered on the same floor as the contenders for the chess championship, Lord Roger Mountbatten and Grant Powell and their parties, though not by any personal choice.

If he had been in another profession, Chan might have remained in Paris for the entire match, but in his capacity as a criminal investigator, he would be fortunate to be able to attend the first six to eight games of the tournament before being called back to duty.

His friend, Claude DeBevre, was a big man, taller and more muscularly heavy. His face had a granite-like cast, now shadowed beneath the widow's peak of his salt-and-pepper hair. His admiration and friendship for Chan, however, had softened his normally stern countenance, and his eyes were a warm blue behind his shell-rimmed glasses.

The two friends entered the Frontenac, and paused just inside the wide double-entrance doors. Too early for a crowd, the high ceilinged lobby seemed imposingly vast and yet discreet in its tasteful furnishings and air of quiet luxury. There was none of the usual administrative noise: no whirring, banging cash registers, no gossiping clerks in cages, only a receptionist, and a concierge, and an occasional porter or page-boy.

Beyond the lobby, to the right of the elevators, was the hotel arcade of boutiques, coiffeurs, travel agency, and cinema. To the left was the lounge, and a bright cabaret which opened only at night; there was also the double tiered L'Odean dining room. The winding staircase which led to the mezzanine, the Grand Ballroom, and the breakfast salon was directly opposite the main entrance.

DeBevre indicated the opening to the lounge. "It has been a full day, and I believe a cognac would go well at this time. I will buy you one, Charlie."

"French cognac is excellent on the palet, but not so excellent, I fear, on my stomach," Chan admitted ruefully. "However, my throat is dry and a glass of milk would be most welcome."

"*Bien*," DeBevre said. "Shall we go into the lounge?"

Charlie Chan nodded, and the two men started across to the entrance. As they did so, a wiry, youthful-looking man entered the lobby from the shop area and crossed to the elevators; at that same moment, the doors of one lift whispered open and the wiry man suddenly stood face to face with a bearish man in his late fifties and a svelte, blonde-haired girl no more than about twenty-one.

The wiry man, who was Raymond Balfour, Grant Powell's friend and adviser, clenched his hands into fists and glared at the older one, ignoring the girl.

"Well, well," he said, "if it isn't Mountbatten's silent partner. On your way to make more trouble, Kettridge?"

Clive Kettridge, Roger Mountbatten's wealthy backer, retorted in as loud and vitriolic a tone, "If anyone's making trouble these days, Balfour, it's you and that damned egocentric Grant Powell!"

Both Chan and DeBevre stopped, turning toward the sound of the angry voices. It was not because they wished to eavesdrop, but because they were trained police officers who sensed immediately that their presence might soon be required in order to circumvent violence or a public disturbance.

"Your protest is sheer insanity," Balfour said angrily. He was intense, dark-haired, with bright brown eyes that were flashing now with rage and indignation. In his early thirties, he wore a modish blue suit and a flowered French cravat. "It's nothing but a cheap attempt to excuse Mountbatten's shoddy playing by casting aspersions on a brilliant young talent like Grant Powell!"

"Rubbish!" Kettridge shouted back. He had a bushy mane of silvering hair and a fat, ruddy-complected face, and was addicted to heavy British tweeds and a long, curved, briar pipe. "You know bloody damn well, Balfour, that Powell couldn't possibly hope to win this tournament without the aid of unethical tactics. And by God, we shan't stand for it! It's a disgrace, an outrage—"

"Father, please," the blonde girl warned. She was Jennifer Kettridge, Clive's only daughter. Dressed in a chic ice-blue pants suit, which matched the color of her eyes, she was stunningly attractive. "You mustn't allow yourself to become upset again." Turning, Jennifer glared at Balfour. "Haven't you said quite enough?"

"Now listen here, Jennifer—" Balfour began.

"Miss Kettridge to you, Mister Balfour. You know, I wouldn't be surprised if you were the one behind the whole nasty business. I simply can't believe Grant would undertake to . . . to cheat on his own."

"Cheat is precisely the word for it," her father growled. "Secret chemicals, electronic equipment—we'll find out exactly what it is. When we do, that will be the end of you and Mr. Grant Powell, Balfour."

Almost as crimson now as the Englishman, Balfour asked in a low, cold tone, "Are you making an official complaint claiming illegalities?"

Kettridge pursed his lips tightly. "Give us another game like the first, and I promise you we shall. We shall have the Grand Ballroom cleared and completely examined by experts. Tables, chairs, floor, ceiling, spectators' seating, everything!"

"Fine," Balfour snapped. "And you won't find a thing, because there's nothing to find. No illegalities, no trickery of any kind. Grant doesn't need any assistance in beating Roger Mountbatten; all he needs is the same sort of brilliant play as he exhibited with his classic Nimzo-Indian defense. I suggest, Mr. Kettridge, that you make your asinine protest, and when the official investigation uncovers nothing, I trust you'll have the good grace to apologize to Grant and to myself—publicly."

When he'd finished speaking, Balfour didn't wait for a reaction or a response; he whirled and stalked off across the lobby, past Chan and Prefect DeBevre, and out of the hotel. Kettridge, his face mottled, stood spluttering impotently for a moment. Then, grasping his daughter's arm, he pulled Jennifer into the elevator, and a second later the lift ascended out of sight.

Chan and DeBevre exchanged glances. The Oriental detective said ruefully, "It would seem that the troubled waters grow more turbulent instead of calm with the passage of time."

DeBevre sighed. "Ah, Charlie, I have always believed that chess was a noble game, one indulged in by gentlemen of discriminating taste, great intellect, and rational outlook. Yet M'sieur Mountbatten and M'sieur Powell act as if they are opposing generals involved in a campaign of war."

"Your analogy is most apt," Chan acknowledged. "Chess was originally conceived as a game of war—the Hindu chaturanga—and has kept its spirit well in modern times. Lord Mountbatten and Mr. Powell are not unique among chess opponents. The British master, Blackburne, once flung Stenitz from a window when the latter defeated him in a match. This was more than one hundred years ago! Tradition, alas, often wears a long beard."

"Well put, Charlie; it does indeed." DeBevre sighed again. "Shall we have our refreshments now, in the lounge?"

"Yes, please."

II

THE TWO police investigators crossed to enter the dark, mahogany-paneled room. Rococo brass fixtures were on the walls, and sumptuous blue velvet covered the booths along one wall as well as the stools arranged before the long bar decorated with fleur-de-lis. Most of the booths were filled, this being the cocktail hour, but there was only the black-jacketed barman and three men at the bar.

Chan and DeBevre stepped up to the mahogany plank, some distance from the trio. In the dim lighting, Chan recognized the tallest of the men as the reporter, Tony Sprague; he also knew the other two, having been introduced to them because of their connection with the Transcontinental Chess Tournament. They were Melvin Randolph, the American just defeated by Powell for the right to meet Mountbatten in the Transcon championship, and Hans

Dorner, the Swiss referee who had presided over the match the night before.

Sprague, a fair-haired man in his late twenties who wore bright red bow ties and an expression of brash, sardonic amusement, was saying, "Well, Randolph, do you believe what Kettridge has been telling people today? That Grant Powell is using some sort of illegal device to distract Mountbatten, to put him off his game?"

Randolph, leaning against the polished brass railing of the bar, frowned deeply. He was dressed expensively and fastidiously—he had a reputation as a fussy individual when it came to his personal appearance—in a charcoal gray suit, lime-green shirt, and handmade silk tie. His well-lined face was freshly shaven, except for a pencil-thin waxed mustache, and if Sprague's expression was one of cynicism, Randolph's seemed to be worried, almost agitated.

"Well," he said, "I don't know. It seems hard to believe . . ."

Dorner—a fiftyish man with a ring of wispy hair around his bald pate and the pale, brittle look of middle-aged efficiency—said: "There has been no official protest registered."

"Not yet," Sprague admitted, "but I've got a feeling there will be, and damned soon. Kettridge has been raving about illegalities since Mountbatten stormed out of the ballroom last night. He's getting himself into a corner where he'll have to follow through."

"But I still can't believe Grant would cheat," Randolph said.

"No? Well, maybe not. But don't forget, Grant Powell was trained in electronics work before turning to professional chess full time. In fact, I understand he was a genius at working with those machines."

"It is impossible that electronic equipment was used in any manner last night," Dorner said sententiously. He scowled into his glass of Pernod. "But I would welcome an investigation nevertheless. At least it will put an end to this foolish talk, and it will prove once and for all that Hans Dorner is a competent referee of tournament chess."

The barman poured a snifter of cognac for Prefect DeBevre and was returning with a glass of milk for Chan as Sprague swiveled on his stool and saw the two police officers.

"Well, Mr. Chan, Prefect DeBevre," he said. "When did you come in?"

"A few moments ago, Mr. Sprague," Charlie Chan answered quietly.

"Then you overheard our conversation?"

"It was unavoidable. One's ears unfortunately are not like one's mouth: they cannot be closed at will."

Sprague laughed. "What's your opinion on the controversy?"

"As an interested spectator only," Chan replied carefully, "I am not in a position to offer a qualified opinion."

"In other words, no comment." Sprague laughed again and then turned to Claude DeBevre. "And you, Inspector?"

"I have no comment either, M'sieur Sprague."

"Well, so much for both sides of the Atlantic," the reporter said with his customary flippancy. He stood up, slapped Randolph on the back, nodded to Hans Dorner, Chan, and DeBevre, and left the lounge.

"I do not think I care for that young man, or his attitude," Dorner said moodily. "Is there not already too much adverse publicity without that man constantly fishing for more?"

Randolph said nothing, still deep in thought. After a moment, he finished his Cointreau and quickly departed.

Dorner ordered another Pernod and brooded into it, obviously not wishing further conversation. Chan honored this since he did not relish further involvement in the pyrotechnics surrounding the tournament. He personally felt Grant Powell was not using illegal methods in his play and that the problems between the rival chess factions could be satisfactorily resolved without further bickering.

But then bickering seemed to be a part of the game. Chess devotees could be as temperamental as opera stars. Chan allowed his thoughts to turn to contemplation of the pleasant day he had spent with DeBevre, and of the evening to come, particularly the evenings' dining.

According to the Prefect, who, like Chan, was an acknowledged expert in matter of haute cuisine, the Hotel Frontenac's chef was one of the best in all of Paris. A friend of the chef's, DeBevre had asked him to prepare one of his several specialties—the choice had been left up to him—in honor of Chan; and as a result, Chan expected the meal in L'Odean to be a memorable one.

III

IN THE EXACT center of the massive Grand Ballroom, which comprised the entire mezzanine of the Frontenac, one of Paris' most luxurious and Gallic hotels, the two grim-visaged men faced one another across that miniaturized battlefield known as a chessboard.

Set along the two high, protracted side walls were specially constructed tiers of seats, similar to those in an American basketball field house where nearly three thousand avid enthusiasts from all over the world had gathered for this, the opening game of the $100,000 Transcontinental Chess Tournament. The great hall was filled with absolute quiet, but there was an electric tension in the air that was almost tangible.

The two players, both seated in leather armchairs, were stiffly motionless as they studied the positioning of the few remaining pieces on the board. The game had begun five hours before, at four p.m. of this warm spring day, and it was now nearing an obvious culmination: victory for one, defeat for the other.

But both victory and defeat would be short-lived; two nights hence, in this same ballroom, the two men would again assemble for a third game—and would continue to meet head-to-head until one of them acquired a total of 12-1/2 points and was crowned the new champion of Transcon chess. It was conceivable that a total of twenty-four games would have to be played in order for this to happen, since each triumph earned one point and each draw one-half point for the respective opponents.

Playing white was the reigning and three-time Transcon champion, Roger Mountbatten, a craggy, outspoken Englishman of middle-age. With his mutton-chop beard and military bearing, he looked more like a retired army major than an expert at the world's most cerebral game.

The challenger, playing black, was an unorthodox and equally outspoken American named Grant Powell, who was half Mountbatten's age and whose rise in the chess world had been meteoric. Powell had thick black hair, worn modishly long, and possessed a smooth boyish face; his normal air was one of genial insolence, though he displayed none of that quality at the present moment.

Seconds continued to tick off on the clock, and the tableau in the center of the ballroom remained frozen. Nearby, Swiss referee Hans Dorner stared at the positioning of the board with an intensity akin to that of the players.

At the closed end of the ballroom, a bilingual Frenchman presided over a muted public address system, ready to announced to the crowd the game's 48th move—which was to be Powell's—as soon as it was made and confirmed by Dorner.

Then, almost lazily, the American challenger leaned forward and moved his king; the gesture was clearly one of insolent triumph, the Powell trademark when he was personally assured of victory. Dorner confirmed the move, the announcer related it in four languages to the crowd, and a ripple of excited murmuring passed through the vast assemblage.

Mountbatten clutched the arms of his chair, and his face began gradually to redden until it was the color of spoiled beef. Staring at the board, he realized—as did some of the more expert members of the audience—that he had been placed in an impossible position, and that the second game now belonged solely to Grant Powell.

According to propriety, he should now stand, extend his hand to the challenger, and officially concede. Instead, to the vocal and shocked surprise of the crowd, Mountbatten jumped explosively to his feet, nearly upsetting the chessboard, and pointed a finger at the American challenger. The extended arm trembled with apparent rage.

"Very good, Powell!" he bellowed. His voice was stentorian in its fury, ringing throughout the ballroom. "Another example of the Nimzo-Indian defense. And yet another example of unethical if not downright illegal chess to boot!"

With those bitter, savage words, Mountbatten spun on his heel and stalked out of the ballroom, through the double entrance doors at the front of the enclosure.

Everyone else in attendance seemed to be stunned—everyone, that is, except Grant Powell. Smiling, his wide mouth quirked insolently, the young chess expert stood up and crossed to the bewildered-looking Swiss official, Hans Dorner. He patted Dorner on the back, then looked at the murmuring sea of faces on both sides of him, raised both his arms in a sign of victory, and walked casually from the ballroom in the wake of his angry opponent.

It wasn't until after both players had disappeared, and Dorner had hurried to the room where officials of the tournament had gathered in conference at the closed end, that the crowd, still buzzing at the unexpected turn of events, began to disperse.

Charlie Chan and Claude DeBevre, as shocked and puzzled as their fellows, made their way down the wide, curving staircase to the Frontenac's lobby and then out into the warm Parisian night. They went to the Champs-Elysées, off which the Frontenac was located, and walked along the tree-lined concourse until they came to one of the numerous sidewalk cafes offering a clear view of the Arc de Triomphe. Sitting at a table there, they ordered cafe au lait and sat sipping it while they discussed what they had recently witnessed.

"But why, Charlie?" DeBevre was saying. "Why would M'sieur Mountbatten make such a public accusation as he did? In private, in a hotel lobby, yes. Rude, but not official. But in front of thousands? And it was an accusation; a man does not use the words 'unethical' and 'illegal' unless he means them."

"No, he does not," Chan admitted with grave concern. "And yet, there appeared to be, nothing unethical or illegal about tonight's contest."

"My opinion, exactly," DeBevre concurred. "M'sieur Mountbatten's words seem totally unfounded—and his actions most unfortunate."

"It would seem so," Chan said. "However, there may be much to which we are not privileged at the moment. Before we judge either Mr. Mountbatten or Mr. Powell, we must wait until more facts are in our possession."

"You are right, of course, Charlie. Still, I cannot help but feel that tonight's display by M'sieur

Mountbatten is yet another of the animosities which have marked the past seven days."

Chan nodded agreement.

DeBevre was referring to the stormy events which had taken place since the arrival of both the Mountbatten and Powell retinues one week earlier. Promoters of the tournament had made the mistake of quartering both parties at the Frontenac, intermingled on the same floor.

From the beginning there had been difficulty. Mountbatten had been quoted in the international press as saying that he had "little respect for Grant Powell, both as a man and as a craftsman of chess"; Powell, in turn, had been quoted as saying that "Mountbatten is washed up as the Number One figure in Transcontinental chess" and that it would require "no more than thirteen games" to achieve the required 12-1/2 points for the unseating of the champion.

Other followers and backers of the two men—such as Mountbatten's business manager and monetary backer, Clive Kettridge; Powell's best friend and adviser, Raymond Balfour; Powell's wife, Laura; and ex-American Transcon champion, Melvin Randolph—had engaged in sniping attacks as well.

Matters had threatened to get out of hand when there was personal and public confrontations between members of the two factions, which were played up in the press; and even though promoters and officials had managed to smooth things over somewhat, the atmosphere at the commencement of the match tonight had been one of open hostility.

Obviously, the argument of the evening before had left Mountbatten smoldering. Else why this public outburst?

Both Charlie Chan and Claude DeBevre were quiet for a time, sipping their coffee and watching the passage of tourists and natives on the narrow, crowded sidewalks of Champs Elysees. Chan's black eyes narrowed as he saw the reporter Sprague approach.

With a dramatic gesture Sprague said, "If you ask me, friends, something's going to happen—tonight or tomorrow—that will shake up the chess world. I don't know exactly what it will be yet, but whatever it is, it'll make international headlines in the bargain."

He seemed happy at the prospect.

Even as Chan and DeBevre exchanged looks, Sprague's prophecy of trouble was beginning to come true.

IV

THE PERSON standing deep in the shadows on the Hotel Frontenac's rooftop terrace, contemplated murder. The gun clenched tightly in the white fist had not yet been fired, but the killer only waited for an opportunity.

Gazing past the now deserted swimming pool, over the parapet of the roof, the killer ignored the starlit skyline of Paris. Silvery in the moonlight, the outdoor pool was surrounded by statues of Venus and mermaids, terrazzo work, and collonades of cerd antique. During the day the guests laughed and swam in the heated water, but now the rooftop terrace was closed for the evening, silent and empty save for the lone individual waiting in tense rigidity under the blackened wing of a temple-shaped cabana.

The weather, even this late in the night, was

mild—the sky so limpid and soft that it enveloped the massive outline of the French capital, giving the impression of small islands captured in the moonshine. It hugged contours huge and high, embracing the deep blue stretches of horizon as well as the dark gray mists wisping mysteriously among the canyons of the streets below.

Paris, seen from these heights, was like a living museum: a city retaining its lingering flair, its sweetness, its magic, despite the lamplit bridges, neon signs, the streams of traffic. One but turned slightly, and it became as it always had been: with finely-worked balconies, the facades of buildings askew, a maze of small lanes and covered passageways and twisting alleys.

In the warm silence a small scraping sound caused the killer to grow more tense with anticipation; it had come from the closed doors that marked the entrance to the roof terrace. The intended victim was coming, and now, at last, the waiting was almost over. Transferring the gun from right hand to left, the watcher reclenched the weapon tightly.

A moment later the doors opened and a masculine figure stepped out onto the roof terrace. The man paused, glancing about the deserted area, not seeing the waiting assassin in the shadows of the cabana.

Methodically, he took a cigarette case from the pocket of his suit jacket, and a lighter flame flare briefly. Smoke drifted up into the dark velvet sky. The man, the victim, stood motionless for a time, smoking; finally, he moved toward the swimming pool, closer to the cabana.

A few more steps, the watcher thought. Just a few more steps. I want to make absolutely sure when I pull the trigger . . .

As if obeying that telepathic command, the man moved along the edge of the starlit pool. Then he stopped, less than twenty yards from the temple-shaped cabana where the murderer hid, and called the killer's name in a soft voice. He called it again, and a third time, and then seemed to shrug; he showed his back, but didn't move away.

Now, the killer thought. Now!

The gun muzzle raised, steadied; slowly, carefully, pressure drew the trigger inexorably back.

And nothing happened; the gun failed to fire.

A cry of frustration was stillborn in the assassin's throat. The trigger was squeezed again, and again. It refused to be drawn back all the way, the mechanism was jammed, and there was no way to unleash the bullet into the back of the unsuspecting victim. After all the preparation and risk that had been gone through to obtain the revolver, it had now proved to be useless.

Damn, Damn! the killer thought savagely. I should have checked it more thoroughly, I should have made sure it would fire! But now it's too late, now what am I going to do? Step out and confront him, perhaps maneuver him over to the parapet and push him off? No, that's too dangerous; there's too much chance of failure. I have to think, I have to plan something else, some other way . . .

The man by the pool lifted his left arm and looked at his watch. He muttered something with apparent irritation and began walking toward the entrance again. He paused one last time, letting his eyes sweep the seemingly deserted terrace, before disappearing through the door.

Sagging limply against the cabana wall, the killer clutched the now useless gun and silently vowed: I won't do it this way next time. I don't even want to be there when he dies. What I need is a very clever method of murder. There'll be plenty of publicity as a result of the Transcon tournament . . . yes, yes, I should have thought of that aspect before, the publicity.

Well, suppose he were to die in a locked room? Oh, how perfect! A locked-room death to puzzle the police completely; that's it, that's exactly it! Chess and a baffling murder what a beautifully ironic combination!

Five minutes passed in complete silence. Then the killer left the shadows and walked across the rooftop terrace, moving resolutely now, a new plan beginning to take shape.

V

CLAUDE DEBEVRE'S eyes were bright with expectation as he and Chan strolled into L'Odean for a midnight supper. He said, "You know, Charlie, that in Paris there is a gourmet society, *Club de la Fourchette Agile*."

"The Quick Fork," Chan translated, amused.

DeBevre nodded. "It holds competition for the most weight gained at one sitting. I believe we may well be in contest for the prize tonight."

Charlie Chan sighed ruefully, patting his girth. "A man's folly should be his greatest secret; but in my case, the secret is out . . ."

A white-frocked Maitre d'Hotel conducted them to their prominently located table, and for a few moments they gazed about the lavish interior, which was decorated in the gold-leaf Belle Epoque style. Then came a bottle of dry champagne as an aperitif, and fresh, succulent brook trout in brown butter. When they had finished this excellent appetizer, the two friends settled back to await the main course.

Shortly, from behind the golden panels concealing the kitchen doors, came a small procession; the Maitre d, a waiter pushing what appeared to be a gleaming stockpot on wheels, and a solemn young busboy laden with a cloth-covered tray. All three came to a halt at a serving cart in front of Chan's and DeBevre's table.

The Maitre d, ceremoniously lifted the lid of the stockpot, revealing a plump Bresse chicken studded with black flecks of truffle. He impaled the bird and held it up for a moment so that Chan and DeBevre could inhale the ambrosial fragrance, bringing murmurs of admiration from the patrons nearby. Then he carved breast, wings, and legs, laid each portion on a mound of rice, coated everything with a creamy golden sauce, and served them while the waiter poured a chilled Meursault into crystal glasses.

The only word Charlie Chan could think of as he tasted the savory chicken was "sublime".

For some time both men were completely involved with their meal. In fact, so involved were they that neither of them noticed the young couple who approached their table until the man said, "Hello, Mr. Chan. Saw you from the entrance and decided we'd come over."

Charlie Chan glanced up, seeing the tall, muscular form of Grant Powell. The American chess champion was wearing his captivating and insolent smile, which, Chan observed, added a certain luster and intensity to Powell's deep-set set eyes and gave him an unsettling impression of being able to read one's mind. The Oriental detective considered what it would be like to sit across a chessboard from those mesmeric Powell features.

"Mind if we join you?" the young man asked.

Despite the blunt intrusion, Charlie Chan smiled graciously. "The flavor of our dinner would be spiced by your presence," he said, "and its beauty enhanced by your wife's. May I introduce Prefect de Police, Claude DeBevre."

"*Enchanté*," DeBevre murmured, rising to shake hands.

"I hope this isn't an imposition," Laura Powell said with a hint of embarrassment.

Almost as tall as her husband, she had burnished, copper-colored hair which fell in loose waves around both shoulders, contrasting startlingly with the jade green of her flaring silk pants-suit. She had the white translucent complexion of a true redhead, relieved only by the scarlet slash of her slightly parted lips and the dark, deep look of perpetual invitation which some women naturally possess.

"It really is my fault," Laura continued, allowing DeBevre to seat her. "I've heard so much about you, Mr. Chan, and when I learned that Grant had met you yesterday, I simply had to make your acquaintance too."

"I am most honored," Chan replied warmly.

Powell signaled for the waiter, and ordered for two: French onion soup, Medallions de Boeuf, and a bottle of Bordeaux. His failure to consult his wife first, as any gentleman ought to have done, seemed to irritate DeBevre, who appreciated good manners and deference toward ladies; but Powell paid him no notice.

"Well, Mr. Chan," Powell said to the Honolulu detective, "you've no doubt heard the accusations those pompous windbags Mountbatten and Kettridge have been making about me. Tell me, do you think they're right and that I cheated today?"

"Grant!" Laura Powell said with a slight blush. "Why do you always have to be so damnably rude and offensive?"

"What's the point of pussyfooting around? I merely asked a question," retorted her husband. "I've nothing to hide."

"Then you have no objections to an investigation, M'sieur?" DeBevre asked, momentarily relieving Chan of the necessity of answering Powell's premature question.

"Of course not. In fact, I welcome it—"

Powell stopped speaking, for at that moment Roger Mountbatten entered the dining room and, in the company of the Maitre d'Hotel, came toward them. Powell's eyes narrowed as he watched the short, ramrod straight figure of the British champion.

The Maitre d seated Mountbatten at a table two away from the one occupied by Chan, the Prefect, and the Powells. The tournament opponents faced one another across the relatively short distance. Then, suddenly, Powell said in a loud voice: "Speak of the devil and he appears. We're in the presence of the soon-to-be dethroned Transcon champion in all his bitter, whining glory."

Laura Powell gasped at the viciousness of her husband's words, and Chan and DeBevre looked disconcerted. It was impossible for Mountbatten not to have heard the slur, and his face congealed with dark anger. Abruptly he stood and came over to the table, glaring hatefully at Powell. Most of the conversation in the dining room had ceased now, and the patrons were nervously eyeing the two men.

"How dare you!" Mountbatten said furiously. "You arrogant young pup! If I were a younger man myself—"

"What would you do, Mountbatten?" Powell asked in calm insolence. "Give me 'six of the best'?"

"Blast you! I'll have you blacklisted throughout the chess world! I'll have you damned well arrested if the investigation proves you've been cheating, debasing the honorable game of chess!"

"So you and Kettridge are going through with

your ridiculous protest after all, are you?"

"We hadn't decided until this moment, but now I fully intend to launch an official complaint. I dislike you more than I've ever disliked anyone, inside or outside of chess. You ought to be flogged, you ought to be—"

"—Shot at sunrise?" Powell finished for him, a half-smile on his lips.

Mountbatten sputtered, couldn't seem to think of anything further to say, and spun abruptly to stalk from the dining room amid the shocked murmurs of the patrons.

"Oh Grant, how could you?" Laura Powell moaned softly. "Why do you always have to make a scene? Why can't you act decently for once in your life? Why can't you grow up?"

"What, and spoil my image?" Powell said. But he seemed to be somewhat subdued now, conscious of the staring eyes around him. If he was not exactly contrite, he was at least having second thoughts about his childish display. Finally he rose. "Excuse me, gentlemen. I think I need a drink more than I need food right now. Coming, Laura?"

"Now that you've succeeded in shaming me, I don't seem to have much choice and I certainly don't have any appetite left. Mr. Chan, Prefect DeBevre—please accept my apologies for my husband's insufferable rudeness." Her voice was subdued but firm.

"Such unfortunate incidents are best and often

quickly forgotten," Chan said tactfully.

"I hope so," Laura replied. She gripped her frowning husband by the arm and strode with him as regally as she was able from the dining room.

"Whatever can be the matter with M'sieur Powell?" DeBevre demanded of Chan. "He is an intelligent man; there is no reason I can see for such actions."

"Youthful intelligence is sometimes a slave to emotions," Charlie replied, "and allows the tongue to rule innate wisdom. A sad saying, but alas a true one."

The two friends returned to their meal; but the previous gastronomic magic had somehow vanished now, and the remainder of their repast was a somber affair, though the excellence of the Frontenac's *haute cuisine* did not go unnoticed.

VI

THE MEAL, as promised, had been sumptuous, a gourmand's delight. Chan appreciated fully each elegant dish as it was served. As always, he was able to concentrate on the pleasant meal, enjoying it thoroughly despite all thoughts about the afternoon's unpleasantness.

Entering his room after dinner, Chan crossed the thick rose-patterned carpet and adjusted the window. It opened easily, without the noisome squeak of old hinges, and overlooked a palm-studded courtyard free of automobiles or scooters with their racket and stench. The curtains were thick and overlapped generously. The remainder of the room was opulent, containing a wardrobe, a dressing table, a writing desk, an easy chair, a telephone on the nightstand, a triptych mirror; the dressing table held only a basket of fruit, complete with a small plate, a paring knife, and a handwritten note reading:

"Welcome to the Hotel Frontenac, Mr. Chan; please let me know if there is anything I can do to make your stay more pleasant. M. Dumont, Manager." The fruit and the note had been personally delivered when Chan arrived.

The room's piece de resistance was the ornate chandelier which hung from the middle of the ceiling. It dominated everything else, a magnificent example of the Empire period, sparkling with diamond-faceted glass baubles, intricately formed of rococo gilt arms wreathed in metal vines and leaves as though overgrown by golden grapes. Frosted globes clustered at each of the many arms, bathing the room in soft, warm light.

And, as Chan noted with pleasure, there was a switch directly above the middle of the bed's headboard which controlled the fixture when one finally wished to douse the light for sleep.

Chan was delighted with the comfort and coziness of the room. Originally he had requested a suite, his usual preference, but because of the chess tournament and because of the general scarcity of Parisian hotel accommodations at all times, none had been available. He was, however, not in the least disappointed with this chamber.

Contentedly, Chan changed into a pair of silk pajamas, hand-dyed in blue-and-gold batik, and slipped between the sheets. The linen was crisp and cool, and Chan leaned back against the pillows, a large but not overly plump Buddha-like figure. It was only then that he allowed himself to think of the events of the past two days.

Chan's mind, always concerned with the human condition, brooded over the volatile words exchanged that afternoon and late evening. Although as a man of intellect he put little faith in premonitions, he had a strange feeling that a tragedy of some kind was soon to mar the Transcon tournament; harsh emotions such as those which had been displayed could all too easily erupt into violence. Sprague's words had hardly helped, nor had the argument later.

Sighing, Chan reached up over the headboard to switch off the chandelier. He lay in the darkness, trying to place his mind at ease so that he could sleep; but the premonition of disaster still lingered. Time passed, and finally he felt himself slipping warmly into slumber.

The sudden explosive sound which woke him and brought him sitting up in bed was muffled, and Chan was not immediately sure what it had been. Massaging sleep from his eyes, he listened intently—and the feeling of tragedy was once again strong inside him.

At first there was only silence, but then from the hallway there came the sound of excited, querulous voices. The Honolulu detective clicked on the chandelier, quickly got out of bed, and put on his robe. Then he opened the door and stepped out into the dimly lit hall.

At the far end, four rooms from his own a small knot of people was clustered before one of the doors. Hurrying down there, Charlie Chan recognized Grant and Laura Powell, Tony Sprague, and Melvin Randolph; and as he reached them, Clive Kettridge and Roger Mountbatten appeared around the corridor well beyond.

"It was a shot, a gunshot!" Laura Powell was saying urgently. "Grant and I heard it clearly!"

"I thought this was your room, Mrs. Powell," Sprague said. "It's the one you and your husband have occupied since you arrived."

"That's right," Powell told "him, "but Laura and I switched rooms with Ray Balfour just before dinner."

"Why would you do that?"

"Because of all the damned trouble Kettridge and Mountbatten have been making over the chess match," Powell snapped angrily, glaring at the two Britishers. "People kept bothering Laura and me, and we got tired of it. There are no other rooms available, and so we simply switched with Ray to get some rest."

While he was listening to this exchange, Chan tried the doorknob and found the door locked. He bent, peering into the latch opening, and saw that the key was in the lock on the inside. There was no sound at all from the room.

Chan turned and said to Sprague, "Please, will you go downstairs and summon the concierge? This door is locked and we must have the key."

"Right, Mr. Chan," the reporter agreed, and hurried off toward the elevators.

"What could have happened?" Laura Powell questioned uneasily. "That was a gunshot we heard!"

"No doubt of that," Kettridge said in a somewhat subdued tone of voice. "I heard it clearly."

"So did I," Mountbatten concurred.

"Did Mr. Balfour have a weapon, that you know about?" Chan asked Grant Powell.

"No, I doubt it. Why would he have a gun? He certainly wouldn't need it here."

Chan looked at the others. "Do any of you possess weapons here in the hotel?"

Everyone denied it in low voices. Charlie Chan nodded once; and since this was his element, the type of situation he had handled so many times in the past, he said authoritatively, "Please stand back from the door, but stay here in the hallway until the room has been opened."

Then he turned and hurried back to his own room. Removing one of the wire hangers from his wardrobe, he bent the loop of the hanger until it was straight. Then he returned quickly to Balfour's locked door, inserted the wire into the latch, and probed carefully. A moment later, he managed to dislodge the key and there was a soft thumping sound as it fell to the carpet inside.

VII

FROM DOWN the corridor, there was the sound of the elevator doors opening; Sprague and the concierge, who looked perplexed and upset, emerged into view. When they reached the group, Chan said, "Have you brought the key?"

"Oui, M'sieur Chan," the concierge answered, mopping his brow and extending a master key to the Chinese detective. "This key opens all chambers in the Frontenac."

Chan used the key on the door. The others crowded in close behind him. The room was shrouded in darkness, but Chan detected the unmistakable odor of spent gunpowder. His fingers moved along the wall inside, found the light switch, and the room was abruptly bathed in soft light.

"Oh!" Laura Powell gasped. She clutched her breast and turned her face against her husband's shoulder.

"Good God!" Melvin Randolph exclaimed.

Raymond Balfour lay sprawled in the middle of the room's double bed, the bedclothes concealing the lower half of his body. The upper half was drenched in blood, and a gaping wound was visible in his chest. One arm was flung lifelessly over the side of the mattress, the other bent and curled around the pillow.

Balfour's face was contorted in an expression of agony, and Chan grimly surmised that the bullet which had struck him had not brought instantaneous death. There had obviously been a few pain-wracked seconds, although not enough for Balfour to have moved from his position on the bed.

"But how . . . how could it have happened?" Mountbatten whispered, his voice shocked. No one answered.

Chan turned to the concierge, who was standing in horrified rigidity inside the door. "I suggest you place an immediate call to Prefect DeBevre. Little doubt exists that the sudden demise of Raymond Balfour falls within his jurisdiction."

The concierge swallowed, blinked, and then nodded. He left the room with the palm of one hand pressed against his forehead in a Gallic sign of distress, muttering, "Oh, that such a thing could happen at the Frontenac!"

"Do you . . . think it was murder, Mr. Chan?"

Kettridge asked.

"It is not the opinion of Charlie Chan which matters," the Honolulu detective stated with his customary modesty. "However, all indications point to murder. This room is identical to mine; also, I believe, to all rooms on the third floor. The single set of windows, as can be seen, are latched securely. The single door was also locked from the inside, with the key in the latch, indicating the victim secured it while alone in the room.

"Also, Raymond Balfour was in bed with the lights off, apparently thinking of sleep and not of death. The weapon which was used to inflict the fatal wound is not to be seen, and the upper chest is hardly the place which a suicide would select."

"But who would want to kill Ray Balfour?" Powell asked with incredulity.

"Maybe Balfour wasn't the intended victim," Sprague said, his eyes bright. "You told us a couple of minutes ago in the hall that you switched rooms with him tonight; did you tell anyone about that switch?"

"No," Powell answered, frowning. "We didn't."

"Then maybe the killer didn't know about it, and somehow Balfour took a bullet intended for you!"

"That's ridiculous!"

"Of course it is," Laura Powell agreed. "No one would want to kill Grant or Ray Balfour. Oh, this is horrible, horrible!"

"What I should like to know," Mountbatten said, "is how anyone could have gotten in or out of this room if the door and the windows were locked from the inside. I say, it's not only puzzling but a bit eerie as well."

"That's not all it is," Sprague said excitedly. "It's also the story of the year. Oh man, will this be a scoop to set the world on its ear! Excuse me, I've got to make a telephone call. I'll be in my room if anybody wants me."

"It is perhaps a wise idea if everyone now returns to his own room," Chan suggested. His voice was soft but imperious—and he didn't add that if there were clues to be found in the murder chamber, the less likely it was that they would disappear or be obliterated if people were not allowed to mill about.

When the others, murmuring among themselves, had departed, Chan closed the door and began a slow and methodical examination of the room. Confirming his earlier observation, he went to the window. It was securely locked. He opened the wardrobe and dresser, looked under the bed, checked the adjoining bathroom; the murder weapon was nowhere to be found. There was no indication of how Raymond Balfour had been shot.

Twenty minutes had passed when a sleepy, shocked Claude DeBevre arrived with a retinue of Parisian gendarmes and laboratory technicians.

"Mon Dieu!" he exclaimed when Chan had finished outlining what had happened. "This is terrible, monstrous! Murder in a hotel such as the Frontenac, murder in the midst of a chess tournament upon which world-wide attention is focused! Ah, I was afraid of something like this after all the bad feelings and savage attacks of the past two days."

"Evil, like venom from a poisonous snake, may find its way into the heart of a prince as well as a peasant," Charlie Chan observed. "And once sown, the seeds of murder may bear bitter fruit any time, any place."

DeBevre sighed. "That is all too true, Charlie. But how could M'sieur Balfour have been killed in a locked room? Where could the murderer have gone, and where is the murder weapon?"

"Too many pieces are still missing for us to be able to put the puzzle together just yet," Chan responded.

"Charlie, you have had much experience in matters such as this," the Prefect said. "I know you are on holiday, but I would be indebted if you would assist in this investigation. If anyone can solve this crime quickly, it is you."

"If it is your wish, the assistance of Charlie Chan may be counted upon."

"*Bien*, that is good to hear." DeBevre said.

The doctor who had accompanied DeBevre and the others from the Paris Prefecture finished his examination of the body, and joined Chan and the Prefect. He spoke rapidly in French, then handed DeBevre a small, bloody object on a piece of tissue.

DeBevre stared at the object for a moment, and then turned widened eyes on the Chinese detective. "Incroyable!" he said. "The doctor found this imbedded in the mattress beneath M'sieur Balfour's body, Charlie. It is what killed him, surely, traveling completely through the upper torso in the region of the heart. If I did not see it with my own eyes, I would scarcely believe it."

He opened his palm, and Chan looked at the object which the doctor had given DeBevre. It was not a bullet, or anything resembling a bullet; perfectly round, silver-colored beneath splotches of blood, it was a piece of solid steel.

A ball bearing!

VIII

CHARLIE CHAN'S inscrutable eyes studied the tiny object for a long moment. "A most incredible tool of murder," he said finally, a frown creasing his smooth Oriental brow.

"But why such a thing as this, and not a bullet?" DeBevre wondered. "It does not make sense."

"Perhaps the nature of the weapon, when discovered, will explain the riddle," Chan said. He looked around the hotel room once again. "But if the weapon is still in this chamber, my eyes simply cannot perceive same."

DeBevre, scowling, followed his gaze. "Nor can mine. But my men are thorough, and possibly they may discover the secret yet—if it is still here to be found."

"We may hope so," Chan said. "Meanwhile, it would seem our presence is not required. I suggest that we question the involved parties, one or more of whom may have knowledge which will shed some light on this matter."

"Oui, an excellent idea," DeBevre agreed. "I believe we should begin with M'sieur and Madame Powell, n'est ce pas?"

Chan nodded, and the two detectives left the room and went next door. Grant Powell answered DeBevre's knock and admitted them silently, his face harried, his eyes troubled. On the double bed, his wife rested with a thin coverlet over her.

"I still can't believe it," Powell said, more subdued than usual in the face of the tragedy. "I know Ray is dead, but I simply can't believe it."

"A terrible shock, I am sure, M'sieur," DeBevre said. He glanced at the bed. "How is your wife?"

"I . . . I'm feeling a little better now," Laura Powell replied. Her face, like her husband's, was drawn. "What can we do for you, Prefect DeBevre, Mr. Chan?"

"To begin," DeBevre told the Powells, "I wish to know more about your exchange of rooms with M'sieur Balfour."

Grant Powell slumped into the room's easy chair. "There's really very little to tell about it. As I said earlier, we switched because Laura and I were being bothered by reporters and curiosity seekers and the like."

"It was accomplished with no one except yourselves, M'sieur Balfour, and the concierge being told of it?"

"Yes, that's right."

"Then it is conceivable that you—or perhaps even your wife—was the intended victim, and not M'sieur Balfour."

"As I told Mr. Chan and the others, that's ridiculous," Powell snapped. "Neither Laura nor myself could possibly have enemies who would hate us enough to commit murder!"

"The extent of hatred is often a most well-guarded secret," Chan remarked quietly.

"Maybe so," Powell said stubbornly, "but I refuse to believe it where Laura and I are concerned."

"You know of no one who might have wished Mr. Balfour dead?"

"No, I don't."

"Were there not many strong feelings over the chess tournament?" DeBevre asked. "Arguments, threats?"

"Oh sure, there were words, but there usually are at events such as the Transcon. You can't think Mountbatten or Kettridge or any of the others would kill Ray Balfour over a chess match! That's quite ridiculous."

"Nevertheless," Chan reminded him, "Mr. Balfour is at the moment dead in a very strange manner, by an equally strange weapon."

"You've found out how Ray was killed?"

"We have," DeBevre said. "He was shot with a ball bearing,"

"A what?"

"Mais oui, a round pellet far more damaging than a pointed bullet."

"A ball bearing," Laura Powell said, and shuddered. "How grotesque!"

"Quite so," Charlie Chan agreed. "The nature of the lethal object demonstrates that whoever killed Raymond Balfour is clever. And a clever murderer, having struck once, would not hesitate to strike again."

"Are we back to that again?" Powell demanded, a disdainful look on his face.

"We are," DeBevre told him. "We cannot rule out the possibility that you or Madame Powell was to be the target of the deadly attack, simply because you do not believe it. It would be a good idea to post a guard to protect you both until this matter has been cleared up."

Powell glared at him with stubborn petulance. "I won't have it!" he snapped. "Neither Laura nor I care to have a policeman constantly underfoot. And besides, nothing more is going to happen—not so far as I'm concerned."

"Madame Powell, do you agree with your husband?"

"Yes, I do," she replied. "We're in no danger, I'm sure of that. But we'll be very careful, of course, and will keep our door locked at all times."

"Raymond Balfour also kept his door locked," Chan reminded her pointedly.

"Well, that's true, of course, but I still don't think Grant or I have anything to fear."

DeBevre sighed. "As you wish. But you are to be very careful until the murderer of M'sieur Balfour has been apprehended."

"Don't worry about that," Powell told him with conviction.

The two detectives left the Powells' room and knocked on the door of the chamber across the hall, where Tony Sprague—having somehow managed to obtain a room on the same floor as the chess principals—was quartered. The reporter answered immediately, his eyes still bright with excitement.

"Anything to report on Balfour's murder?" he asked, admitting Chan and the Prefect.

DeBevre explained about the ball bearing, and Sprague's eyes widened. "So now you've got a locked-room murder and a damned unusual weapon to boot. This has to be the biggest story of the year!"

"A violent death is hardly cause for rejoicing," Chan pointed out mildly.

"True enough," Sprague agreed. "But from what I knew of Balfour, I don't think his death is any great loss."

"Why do you say that?"

"He had a reputation as a ladies' man—quite a

reputation. Didn't you know that?"

DeBevre frowned. "No, I did not."

"Well, it's true, all right. There was something of a scandal back in the States not too long ago, where Balfour was caught fooling around with another man's wife. I also have it on pretty good authority that he's been trying to move in on Jennifer Kettridge. I don't think she fell for his line, but I'm not sure.

"Anyway, I know old man Kettridge didn't like the idea much. He warned Balfour about it. I happened to overhear their conversation a couple of days ago."

"Most interesting," Chan said encouragingly.

"I suppose so," Sprague said, "but the way it seems, with that room switch and all, it was Powell who was the intended victim and not Balfour. Murderer still could be Kettridge, though; the two of them obviously dislike one another to the point of hatred. Same thing with Mountbatten. And, after that little talk the two of you heard in the lounge this afternoon, I'd say Melvin Randolph might be a suspect too."

The Chinese detective chose to change the subject. "You were awakened by the shot tonight?"

"Hell, yes," Sprague answered. "It sounded like a cannon going off. Have you got any idea how that ball bearing was fired; from what kind of gun or weapon?"

"Not as yet," DeBevre replied. "When you entered the hallway, M'sieur, had anyone else appeared?"

"The Powells were coming out of their room," the reporter said.

"Did you see anything else?"

"Nothing. I didn't hear anything else, either."

IX

LEAVING Sprague's room, Chan and DeBevre spoke to Melvin Randolph next. The American ex-champion seemed much more agitated than he had earlier that afternoon, but he had nothing new or helpful to tell them. He had entered the hall after being aroused by the gunshot, and had arrived seconds after the Powells and Tony Sprague. He had not heard anything other than the shot, he said. His face registered surprise at the news that a ball-bearing had killed Balfour.

But he could not offer any suggestion as to how it could have been fired. He claimed not to have previously known about the room switch between the Powells and Balfour, and said that he knew of no reason why either of the two men would be marked for murder.

"I suppose," Randolph said somewhat stiffly,

"that after the conversation in the lounge today, you think I might hate Powell enough to want him dead—that I hold a grudge against him for defeating me in the U.S. playoffs. But I could never kill."

Randolph had nothing else to say, so Charlie and the Prefect left and rounded the ell in the corridor. When DeBevre knocked on the door to the suite belonging to Clive and Jennifer Kettridge, it was the lovely young daughter who admitted them.

As they entered, they saw Roger Mountbatten standing beside Kettridge at a silver cart containing several bottles of liquor and mix. Both men came over to greet the two detectives, carrying glasses of what appeared to be whiskey-and-soda. From the expressions on their faces, they looked as if they'd needed the drinks to calm somewhat shaky nerves.

Despite an obvious attempt to appear clam and collected, Jennifer, too, seemed badly upset. Her chin quivered slightly and her eyes were puffed and red-rimmed. She said, after Chan had introduced the French Prefect: "Father told me what happened to poor Raymond Balfour. I . . . I couldn't believe it at first. It's so frightening!"

"Murder," DeBevre said solemnly, "is always frightening."

Mountbatten said, "Has anything new developed? Has the killer been uncovered yet?"

"I'm afraid not, M'sieur. The mystery has, in fact, deepened." DeBevre studied the Englishman critically. "There were sharp differences between you and the deceased, n'est ce pas?"

"A few," Mountbatten admitted reluctantly. "But the differences were over the tournament, and hardly sufficient to result in murder!"

DeBevre then looked at Kettridge. "And you, m'sieur, did you not have a violent argument with M'sieur Balfour in the lobby this afternoon?"

Kettridge worried his lower lip, obviously discomfited. "Yes, it's so. But what Roger said is also applicable to myself. I did not hate the young man enough to wish him dead, and certainly not because of an argument over the tournament."

"Perhaps you had other reasons for disliking Mr. Balfour?" Chan asked. "Perhaps very personal reasons?"

"What do you mean by that remark?" Kettridge demanded.

"We have been informed of Raymond Balfour's appreciation of your daughter's charms, and of your disapproval."

"I will say it's true enough that Raymond tried to press his attentions on me," Jennifer injected quickly, before her father could reply. "They were . . . unwanted. Father disapproved of Raymond, but as there was nothing between Raymond and myself, he would have hardly stooped to murder, would he?"

Kettridge pursed his lips. "What Jennifer says is quite right. I didn't care for Balfour as a suitor, but since she rejected him on her own, I had no cause to hate the man for having attempted to court her. He was a trifle insistent, I must admit, but Jennifer made it quite clear that she wanted nothing to do with him."

DeBevre produced the steel ball-bearing, explaining that it was the object which had killed Balfour. The three Britishers stared at it in wonder, and after a protracted moment, the Prefect said firmly: "I would like to know where each of you were when this was fired. M'sieur Mountbatten?"

"Naturally, I was in my room," the British chess champion answered stiffly. "Mr. Chan can testify to that."

Chan moved his head negatively. "I can testify only to the fact that you and Mr. Kettridge arrived in the hall as I approached. You were in your room prior to the shot?"

"Yes, although I'm afraid I can't prove that. I was alone after Hans Dorner left, about fifteen minutes earlier."

"Hans Dorner!" DeBevre exclaimed. "Why was he in your room?"

"He came to discuss the protest Clive and I lodged against Grant Powell this evening. He was not at all happy about it, I must say."

"Did he say where he was going when he left you?"

"He did not. I suppose he returned to his room.

It's the one directly over Balfour's, on the fourth floor."

DeBevre nodded, then turned to Clive Kettridge. "And you, M'sieur? You were in your room at the time of M'sieur Balfour's death?"

"Why, yes. I was reviewing some chess magazines."

"And I was here with him," Jennifer said. "When we heard the shot, Father jumped up and told me to stay here while he investigated. Terrible—oh, it's all so terrible!" Tears welled in her eyes, and she tried to blink them back.

"For a man you apparently disliked," Chan observed gently, "you mourn in the fashion of a widow."

"It . . . It's not that I disliked Raymond Balfour—or liked him, either. It's just that all death is terrible, frightening."

Chan continued to study her for a moment, wondering about the girl's motives. Was she reacting with the over-emoting of an adolescent? Or were there deeper motivations to her sadness?

Mountbatten was still staring at the bearing in DeBevre's palm. "I don't understand at all how that should have killed Balfour. It was a gunshot we heard, I'm quite positive of that. What sort of gun could fire a ball bearing?"

"No gun at all," Kettridge said. "Not that it matters, of course, since none of us has a weapon. Do we, Roger?"

Mountbatten seemed to hesitate briefly, and then said, "No, I'm sure none of us do."

"Of course not," Jennifer added, and averted her eyes. Chan observed the downward shift of her gaze, and wondered again if perhaps the girl were lying for some hidden reason. But at this point in the investigation, it was too early to tell for certain.

Kettridge stepped up to his daughter and placed an arm about her shoulders. His voice was stern and paternal as he queried the two detectives, "Have you any more questions? Jennifer is upset, as we all are—and it is quite late."

"I have no more questions at this time," DeBevre told him. "Perhaps in the morning."

"Yes, quite so."

Chan and the Prefect returned to the murder room, where the laboratory men had finished their examination and the body of Raymond Balfour had been removed. DeBevre spoke with one of his men, then reported to Charlie Chan that the search had yielded nothing of fresh interest. The carpet had been vacuumed, as was standard procedure, and the contents of the bag would be inspected at the Prefecture.

DeBevre ordered that the room be locked up until further notice, and then he and Chan stepped into the corridor. The Honolulu detective said: "I suggest we visit Hans Dorner. His whereabouts at the time of the shooting are as yet undetermined."

"I was about to make the same suggestion, Charlie," DeBevre agreed.

They rode up one floor in the cage lift, and walked to Dorner's room. The Prefect rapped loudly on the paneling several times, but there was no response.

DeBevre stroked his jaw thoughtfully. "It is now well past midnight, and yet Herr Dorner is still not in his room. Where could he have gone after he left M'sieur Mountbatten's chamber?"

"Your question is at present rhetorical," Chan noted. "When he is located, we will have the answer."

"I will have him located," the Prefect promised. He sighed. "Ah, but it appears this will be a long night. There is little point in both of us going without rest, Charlie. If you wish to retire, I will contact you the moment there are developments."

"It is perhaps best. My brain remains alert, but my venerable body demands rest. I fear it is to my body that I must yield."

Chan bid DeBevre good-night in the elevator, departed on the third floor and returned to his room. Wearily, he removed his robe and slipped into bed again. He lay deep in thought for a long while, reviewing the events of the evening, and then gratefully allowed sleep to claim him.

X

THERE WERE no calls from DeBevre or any other disturbances to interrupt his slumber, and Charlie Chan awoke at eight the following morning feeling thoroughly refreshed. He called room service to request his morning tea and the French croissants for which he had acquired a fondness, and five minutes later there was a knock on the door. Chan, dressed in his silk robe, admitted a porter with his Continental breakfast on a tray.

Charlie Chan sipped his tea and debated calling DeBevre to ask if there had been any further developments. He decided against it, finally, reasoning that the Prefect would have kept his promise to phone if there were any news. Finishing his tea and the last of the croissants, the Oriental detective lay back on the bed again and gazed thoughtfully at the ceiling, once more lost in contemplation.

After a time something seemed to be trying to intrude on his consciousness. He concentrated, and suddenly he realized what was bothering him. Quickly he dressed in one of the tailored double-breasted suits with wide lapels and cuffs that he favored, combed his straight black hair, smoothed his neatly trimmed Chinese mustache, and left the room to immediately enter one of the elevators. In the lobby, he spoke with the haggard concierge, who was still on duty, requesting a key that would open the door of the murder room.

"But Prefect DeBevre ordered that the room remain locked," the concierge argued. "No one is to enter, not even members of the hotel staff."

"It is my humble opinion that Prefect DeBevre would have no objection to me entering. Please call him and inquire, if you are doubtful."

The concierge gnawed the inside of his cheek thoughtfully, and finally demurred, saying: "Perhaps a call is not necessary, M'sieur Chan. The Prefect did tell me, it seems, that you were to help him with his investigation."

He relinquished the master key, and Charlie Chan went up to the third floor again and let himself into the room in which Balfour had met his mysterious end. He spent five minutes examining the room, noting a few small flecks of gilt paint on the carpet; after another five minutes, the Honolulu detective had confirmed his hunch—and knew, or at least suspected, how Balfour had been murdered.

Chan also was aware that someone had been in the room since it had been locked the night before; and that this person had removed the contrivance which had been used to fire the lethal ball bearing.

Hurriedly Chan left the chamber, relocking the door, and started down the corridor. To his surprise, Jennifer Kettridge was waiting in front of his room, tears shining in her eyes.

"Oh, Mr. Chan," she said, "I was hoping to find you!"

"You appear upset," Chan observed; then, in a very soft voice, he asked: "Would this perhaps be because of your untruths last night?"

"Then you . . . you knew?"

"A detective cannot read minds, but sometimes faces may reveal much. Lies are like blemishes, for often they cannot be hidden."

Jennifer reflected bitterly: "It is not I who is suffering, so much as it is my father. Prefect DeBevre discovered that I hadn't been in the room with Father as I'd said, but downstairs in the cabaret. I should've thought of the chit I'd signed, that it would give me away even if I weren't recognized. But everything was happening so quickly. I . . . I only wanted to help!"

"Wisdom is not always present when affection speaks. I presume, then, that Mr. Kettridge was alone in your room?"

"Yes." Jennifer lowered her head. "And because of my lie, it looks even blacker for Father, now that it's known he owns a gun, and that it was here with him at the hotel."

"Oh?" Chan's face was expressionless.

Jennifer nodded in confirmation, her blue eyes soft and moist with worry. "It was the sidearm he carried during the War," she explained. "He's always packed it with him on trips, ever since he was robbed in Algeria some years ago, during a tournament."

"And where is this gun at present?"

"That's why Father didn't admit to owning it. You see, he told me after you left that the pistol has been missing from the room for the last two days. Someone obviously stole it, but he didn't report the theft, fearing publicity. When he discovered that Raymond had been shot, he knew it would appear worse for him so he lied, and Roger and I backed him up."

"How did Prefect DeBevre discover this truth?"

"A chambermaid," Jennifer told him. "During his questioning of the hotel staff, she recalled seeing it among Father's belongings in a suitcase he'd inadvertently left open one morning."

"And now your father has been confronted?"

The young girl nodded. "We were eating breakfast in the salon when Prefect DeBevre burst in on us. He allowed me to leave and I came straight to find you. He must still be in the salon with Father, and I'm quite sure he believes Father somehow murdered Raymond."

"Was a motive mentioned while you were present?"

"No. But I suppose the Prefect believes it's either due to the difference of opinion over the Transcon tournament or because of me. Both are utterly ridiculous, of course. Father becomes quite excitable over chess, but he isn't a man of violence.

"And he knew there was nothing between Ray and myself. I never cared for him at all, not with his arrogance. His treatment of women was deplorable as well—as if they were toys to be trifled with and then discarded."

Jennifer looked up again, imploringly. "Father did not kill him, Mr. Chan; I know he didn't! Please help him, please!"

"I may assist only in the capture of a murderer," Chan said gently. "It may be hoped the success of that venture will reaffirm your faith in your father."

"It will, because he's innocent. Find the real killer quickly, Mr. Chan, for Father's sake and . . . and for Grant's, too."

"For Mr. Powell's sake?"

More flushed than ever now, Jennifer realized what she had said. Confusedly, she attempted to explain away her slip. "I . . . well, that is, it was Grant . . . I mean, it was Mr. Powell . . . who might have well been the intended victim, mightn't it? His life might perhaps still be in danger."

Charlie Chan studied her for a moment, and then said, "You care for Mr. Powell—is that not so, Miss Kettridge?" His voice was without censure.

Jennifer sighed. "All right, it's quite useless trying to hide it any longer at least from you, Mr. Chan. Yes, I'm in love with Grant. I have been for quite some time now."

"And does he reciprocate this love?"

"He hardly knows I exist. He's of course happily married and I . . . oh, I simply could never tell him how I feel, under the circumstances. You are the only one who knows my heart, Mr. Chan."

"Then your secret shall remain safe." Charlie Chan smiled reassuringly turned to step away, and then as an apparent afterthought he asked: "Would you tell me, Miss Kettridge, if your father was in your suite all of last evening?"

"All night? Why, of course. We retired soon after you and Prefect DeBevre left us. Why do you ask?"

Chan shrugged, as if the matter were unimportant. "A detective is always filled with much curiosity, about many things," he said enigmatically. "Please excuse me."

XI

CHARLIE CHAN entered his room to wash, and then walked downstairs to the mezzanine and stepped inside the ornate breakfast salon that was reserved for the hotel patrons. It consisted of clusters of small tables filled with guests; a longer table against the far wall that had on it ironed copies of such Parisian newspapers as Le Monde and Figaro, and a decor of murals depicting the palace of Versailles and its gardens.

Toward the back, Chan could make out the hunched form of Claude DeBevre, straddling a wicker chair with his arms folded across its top. He was talking intently to Clive Kettridge, who seemingly had lost interest in his half-eaten breakfast of eggs and bacon.

"M'sieur," DeBevre was saying as Chan approached, "you tell a tale of a missing Webley pistol, when now it is convenient to do so! You ask me to believe you, but can you blame me if I doubt instead?"

Kettridge dabbed his perspiring forehead with his napkin. "I fail to see how it makes one whit of difference in any case! Raymond Balfour was killed with a bearing, not by a bullet, and certainly not by a bullet from my stolen gun!"

DeBevre, who by this time had seen Chan approaching them, gestured with an open hand in the other detective's direction. "Mais oui, but to borrow some of M'sieur Chan's wisdom, liars and criminals often occupy the same dwelling place."

"Out with it, then!" Kettridge jumped to his feet, thumping the table with the knuckles of one clenched fist. "Are you or are you not officially charging me with murder?"

Chan approached quickly. "Please excuse my intrusion," he said. "Before words fly without benefit of thought, I suggest a moment of reflection. Please resume your seat, Mr. Kettridge."

The Englishman stood trembling for a moment, and then capitulated, subsiding once more into his chair. "Yes, I dare say you're right, Mr. Chan. But I shan't condone being called a common criminal, by inference or in any other manner. I shan't!"

DeBevre said to Chan, "I should have summoned you immediately, Charlie, when I learned of this fresh development. But in my zealousness, I neglected to do so. We have perhaps found, as you say, the first break in the case."

Charlie Chan nodded. "I was informed of Mr. Kettridge's missing weapon by his daughter only moments ago."

"Perhaps I was foolish last evening," Kettridge said. "I admit that, in fact. But I insist my missing Webley has nothing whatsoever to do with Raymond Balfour's death."

"That remains to be seen," DeBevre told him. "You still claim also that you did not leave your room prior to the murder? That you ventured forth only to investigate the show?"

"Yes. It's the bloody truth."

"Then, M'sieur, you would not object to a search of your possessions?"

"On the contrary," Kettridge said acidly, "I demand it. Perhaps, when you find nothing, you will think twice about attempting to involve me in this crime."

"Do you wish to accompany us while we conduct this search?"

"I do not." Kettridge stood and stalked from the salon.

Charlie Chan said to the Prefect, "I suggest a search of all suspects' rooms. And perhaps men to watch the exits of the hotel, should anyone connected with the case attempt to leave."

"My men have been here all night," DeBevre told him. "No one who knew Mr. Balfour attempted to leave. Alas, many tried to enter—most of them reporters. M'sieur Sprague's story of the murder has all of Paris, and apparently the entire world, in a ferment." The Prefect expelled a soft breath, shaking his head. "He exercised no restraint whatsoever, unfortunately."

Chan said, "It is fortunate that a policeman of your capabilities is handling such a difficult case."

DeBevre's eyes reflected pride at the compliment, then sobered again due to the gravity of the situation. The two detectives then left the salon and proceeded up to the third floor once again. Jennifer, who had returned to the suite occupied by her and her father, admitted them and offered no objections to a search.

The search yielded nothing in the way of evidence.

Chan and DeBevre then went to Roger Mountbatten's chamber. He did not answer their knock, but with the concierge's master key, they gained entry.

"This is highly illegal," the Prefect warned, slightly nervous at entering without a proper warrant.

"But necessary," Chan responded. "Time is now a most valuable commodity and cannot be wasted."

"You are thinking of something in particular?"

"Of many things," Chan said noncommittally. "Before I put voice to them, I would prefer more facts, however. A song without a melody is only a harsh noise."

They found nothing of interest in Mountbatten's room. Refusing to say more about his suspicions, and not divulging that he had visited the murder room earlier that morning, Chan next accompanied DeBevre in a search of first Tony Sprague's and then Melvin Randolph's chambers. Nothing was found of importance in either chamber. After leaving Randolph's room, the two detectives knocked on Powell's door, and in a few moments, Grant Powell ushered them in, clad only in a towel and wet from a shower.

"Go right ahead," he said after they'd requested permission to search. "If you don't mind, though, I'll dress while you do."

"How is your charming wife this morning?" Chan asked him.

"Much better after some sleep. She's gone downstairs to the lobby for a copy of the *Herald Tribune*, and should be back shortly." Powell sighed and looked almost contrite. "I was something of an ass last night, wasn't I? In more ways than one."

Chan and DeBevre were silent.

"I don't know what makes me act as I do sometimes," Powell said. "Ego, I suppose, and a perverse streak. I'm usually sorry, afterward."

He looked at the two detectives steadily. "As you no doubt know, the tournament has been postponed indefinitely. But I for one want it to continue as soon as Ray Balfour's murderer is caught. One reason is selfish: to prove to the world that I have not been cheating, that I am capable of winning the Transcon championship on merit alone. The other reason is somewhat less selfish. I believe Ray would have wanted me to continue, and to win. He may have had his faults, but he was a good friend, and he truly believed in me and my abilities."

Chan surmised that Powell was revealing depths of integrity and compassion which had previously been buried completely; his opinion of the young chess expert went up considerably.

"I believe your reasons are valid ones, Mr. Powell," he said.

"Thank you." Powell smiled faintly. "I . . . well, thank you."

Charlie Chan and the Prefect soon finished their search of the Powells' room, where they also discovered nothing of importance.

When they had entered the corridor again, Chan suggested, "Perhaps our next stop should be the room of the Swiss chess official, Hans Dorner. We must still ascertain his location last night."

"I questioned him extensively this morning," the Prefect said, "and Dorner claimed that he was upset over the protest which Mountbatten and Kettridge had planned to lodge against Grant Powell. He claims he spent the entire evening at a bistro on the *Champs Elysees*, following his departure from Mountbatten's room."

"Most interesting," Chan said.

"He was not too intoxicated to profess shock and horror at the news of Raymond Balfour's murder."

"What time did he return?"

"Shortly past three that morning. The man at the desk remembers him."

"You have checked his alibi?"

"My men are doing so now."

As the two detectives started from the elevator on the fourth floor, DeBevre said, "I trust Herr Dorner had the good sense to remain in his room, as I instructed him to do. I am far from satisfied with his explanation, and I—"

His words were abruptly cut off by a high-pitched scream from the floor above. It was a chilling, piercing shriek filled with decibels of horror, and it raised the hairs on the back of Charlie Chan's neck.

XII

CHARLIE CHAN and the Prefect exchanged startled glances; then, as the chilling scream continued to echo through the quiet halls, the two men turned and ran back into the waiting elevator. DeBevre punched the button for the next floor, and the cage seemed to rise with impossible slowness.

When it arrived at the fifth floor landing, Chan and DeBevre rushed into the hallway. It appeared deserted in both directions; but the scream sounded again, coming from beyond the ell to their left. They ran down there and turned the corner. A black-and-white uniformed chambermaid was backed against one of the walls, her hands clutched in front of her, her eyes protruding with horror as she stared into the open doorway of one of the chambers. Her screams had brought a small cluster of guests, who milled about and stared with horrified expressions into the room.

As they drew abreast of the doorway, Chan had his first glimpse at the object of the woman's cried and he felt his own stomach contract. He had seen blood and death many times before, but he had never grown inured to it.

The man lying doubled up on his side on the carpeting had a small paring knife thrust between his ribs, near his heart, and there was a vast quantity of blood on the front of his white shirt, on the carpet where he sprawled, and in a sticky crimson trail extending well into the chamber.

In his right hand was clutched an old Webley revolver. He was still alive, his left hand clawing feebly at the nap of the carpet, and his mouth moving soundlessly. But from the position and depth of the wound, and the amount of lost blood, Chan knew death was but seconds away.

The man was Tony Sprague.

Both Charlie Chan and the Prefect knelt beside the dying wire-service reporter, DeBevre calling over his shoulder in French for somebody to phone a doctor. Sprague's eyes were half-rolled up in their sockets, but he seemed to recognize Chan; his free hand came up imploringly, and his lips attempted to form words.

The Honolulu detective bent closer, straining to hear. At first there was no sound save for the excited murmurings of the gathered patrons, plus the now-hysterical sobbings of the chambermaid. Then, in a barely audible whisper, Sprague managed to gasp:

"Checkmate!"

That strange term was all the fatally wounded reporter was able to say. His eyes rolled the rest of the way up in their sockets, and his hand fell back to the carpet. He was dead.

DeBevre looked at Charlie Chan. "What did he say? I could not hear."

Chan repeated Sprague's dying exclamation.

"You are certain?"

"Doubt in this instance does not exist."

"But what could he have meant? I do not understand; I do not understand at all." Grimly, DeBevre turned and crossed to where the chambermaid stood trembling. Speaking to her in soothing French, he managed to calm her sufficiently so that she was able to answer a few questions in a halting, quivering voice.

When she had finished, DeBevre said to Chan, "She tells of coming down the hall with her cart, about to clean the rooms on the opposite side of the hotel. She heard moaning sounds from this chamber and unlocked the door. She saw M'sieur Sprague lying as he is now, and it was then she began to scream."

"She saw no one else in the hallway?"

"No, she insists she did not," DeBevre replied.

"Unlocked the door . . ." Chan said aloud, reflectively; then he asked, "Who is registered in this room?"

"According to the maid it is vacant!"

Chan frowned slightly. "She is certain of this?"

DeBevre spoke again to the chambermaid, who shook her head vehemently and answered in her stronger voice. The Prefect translated to Chan, saying, "She insists it is so. She herself made up this room earlier, in preparation for a new arrival, and it is for this reason she found most surprising the sounds which came from inside, and thus opened the door."

Chan nodded, looking again at the body of the reporter. "We know now," he said grimly, "the nature of the murder weapon."

"How do we know this?" DeBevre asked.

"The knife is similar to one in my room, which came with a complimentary basket of fruit. The vacancy to which the maid referred is only temporary, it would seem, and the basket with this knife was placed here by her this morning. Has she any idea why or how Mr. Sprague was locked in the empty room?"

DeBevre passed a hand over his face and once again questioned the woman. "She has never seen M'sieur Sprague before," he related to Chan a moment later. "She has no idea what he was doing there, and swears she locked the door securely when she was finished earlier."

The Prefect then turned to the group of people and began to question them, but it was obvious by the tones of their voices and the shakings of their heads that they had nothing to add. He told the guests to return to their quarters, and dispatched the chambermaid, who was still in a state of agitated shock, with a warning he might wish to speak to her again later.

Chan by this time was once more kneeling beside the body. Then he rose, using a pencil to hold the Webley pistol by its muzzle, having taken it from the reporter's limp grasp. He began to examine it, careful not to smudge any fingerprints it might contain.. He was about to call something to DeBevre's attention when the hotel doctor and a different but acutely upset concierge rounded the hallway ell.

DeBevre spoke to the concierge while the doctor officially pronounced Tony Sprague deceased. Then the Prefect turned to Chan.

"The concierge confirms the maid's story, Charlie. A Canadian couple is expected shortly, and she was ordered to prepare the room for their arrival." DeBevre glanced down at the body with grim dissatisfaction. "Another murder, this time with an enigmatic dying message. Surely this murder is connected with the killing of Raymond Balfour last night!"

"But this death was not as carefully planned as before," Charlie Chan said. "This was done with sudden decision, and its execution made in haste."

"It would seem so," DeBevre agreed, and then in a low, cold tone, he added: "The haste of a man such as M'sieur Kettridge, perhaps? Is that not his allegedly missing weapon you are holding, Charlie? Perhaps it was not missing at all, and M'sieur Kettridge murdered M'sieur Sprague!"

Chan meditated for a moment, not speaking.

DeBevre went on: "Perhaps M'sieur Sprague was lured here to this vacant room while we were busy downstairs. What more perfect rendezvous for a private confrontation than here, especially if M'sieur Sprague knew something about the death of M'sieur Balfour, and had therefore to be silenced."

"Quite possible," Chan admitted. "This murder is indeed a vicious relative of Raymond Balfour's death, but the exact lineage is still in doubt. The presence of this pistol is more vexing a question than its ownership, however, and the answer may lead to a different direction."

"What do you mean, Charlie?"

Chan indicated the revolver. "It has not been fired. A shot was not heard, the barrel is cool, and the inside is slightly rusted. Yet the cylinder contains bullets. How strange that it was not used."

"Ah, *bien entendu!* If M'sieur Sprague had the gun when he was attacked, why did he not use it to defend himself? And if the killer had possession of it, why was the knife used instead?" DeBevre took off his glasses and wiped the lenses thoughtfully with a handkerchief. "For that matter, why is the gun here at all? I would think the killer would have taken it with him."

"The only explanation which comes to my mind at present," Chan replied, "is that the killer did not wish to keep the weapon on his person and had no other quick way of disposal here in the hotel."

Using a handkerchief, Chan gingerly broke the cylinder, dropping the six stubby bullets into his other palm. "I believe that if you examine the firing mechanism," he said after a moment's inspection, "you will see why the weapon was not used."

"Is it somehow defective?" the Prefect asked.

"It would appear so," Chan said, handing the gun to the Prefect. He studied the bullets next, juggling them in his hand one at a time, and then gave them to DeBevre. "I also suggest a laboratory check of these. The weight of two of them seems less than the others, indicating that perhaps the powder has been removed."

"Mon Dieu!" DeBevre exclaimed. "A gun that will not fire, bullets that cannot work, not one but two locked-room murders! We have no idea how M'sieur Balfour was killed, or how admittance was gained either to his chamber or to his one. *Incroyable!"*

The Prefect looked at the concierge and spoke with harried irritation. The concierge, with widened eyes, then hurried away and DeBevre turned back to Chan. "He is to phone the Prefecture, and soon my men will be here. When they are, I will confront M'sieur Kettridge once more, and this time I will settle for nothing less than the whole and complete truth!"

"Most humply suggest that you assemble all of the interested parties," Chan said. "We may yet find valuable information in the whereabouts of each at the time of this second death."

"Excellent idea, Charlie. I will clear the breakfast salon and use it as my office. It will hold all those concerned quite comfortably."

Chan nodded. "I will meet you there shortly."

"Are you not waiting with me?" DeBevre asked, somewhat bemused.

"I am afraid that this detective's curiosity is a matter of impatience," Chan replied. "As in the sport of kings, a hunch must be played in the fever of the moment."

Leaving the Prefect in a state of bewilderment, Charlie Chan hurried down the hall on his unexplained mission.

XIII

IT TOOK less than an hour for Claude DeBevre to assemble the seven suspects in the breakfast salon. All had been in various parts of the hotel, and all had apparently shown genuine surprise and horror when told of Tony Sprague's murder.

When all seven were seated at the small tables at the rear of the salon, the Prefect leaned against a longer table facing them. His attention was focused on Clive Kettridge, for he was now more than ever convinced that the Britisher was his man.

He said, "So, M'sieur Kettridge, you attempted to leave the hotel not so long ago."

"And what is so incriminating about that? I wished to get a haircut."

"There is a barber downstairs in the arcade," DeBevre told him pointedly.

"I am well aware of that," Kettridge snapped. "I

wanted a British trim, and there is a quite acceptable shop I often frequent nearby."

"My men report you were quite abusive to them."

"Well, I found it distinctly irritating to be prevented from leaving as I chose."

DeBevre smiled without humor. "Perhaps this was your reason, and perhaps not. Again, there is the matter of your gun—the Webley which you claim was stolen from your room."

"It *was* stolen!"

"This, too, remains to be seen. The fact is, however, that we now have the weapon. It was in M'sieur Sprague's hand when he died."

Murmurs of surprise rippled through the assemblage. DeBevre motioned for silence. "*Mais oui,* clutched in M'sieur Sprague's hand—unfired and perhaps in defective condition. We will know more of this when my men at the laboratory have examined the weapon; and we will also know the answer to another mystery surrounding the gun."

"What mystery is that?" Melvin Randolph asked.

"I do not wish to discuss it at present," The Prefect said. He was still stonily regarding Kettridge. "So, M'sieur, there is the fact that you attempted to leave the hotel when you were instructed to remain here, and there is the matter of your gun. There is also the fact that you were not with your daughter prior to M'sieur Balfour's death last night, nor were you with her at the time of M'sieur Sprague's death today."

"No," Jennifer interrupted angrily, "and I was also alone on both occasions. Why don't you accuse me of the murders?"

"I accuse no one—yet," DeBevre said. "Where were you one hour ago, Mademoiselle Kettridge?"

"Where you found me: in our suite."

"And you, M'sieur Kettridge?"

"In the bloody bar. It was rather crowded, and I don't suppose the barman will remember. But I was there, and damn you if you think otherwise!"

The Prefect decided to determine the whereabouts of the other suspects at the time of Sprague's death, before continuing his interrogation of Kettridge. He turned to Roger Mountbatten and asked the question.

"On the rooftop terrace. I had gone up there after breakfast, which was quite early this morning, and I was enjoying the view from a chaise lounge. I came down shortly before you knocked on my door. As to whether or not I was seen, I have no idea. And like Clive, I resent your constant badgering!"

DeBevre ignored this last comment and looked at Melvin Randolph. "And you, m'sieur?"

"I was looking through the boutiques in the arcade, considering among other things the purchase of a new sports coat."

"All morning, m'sieur?"

"Yes, as a matter of fact. Browsing, mostly. What else is there to do, since you have the hotel sealed off like a tomb?"

"Mr. Randolph was there, as he says," Laura Powell said. "I saw him as I came out of the drugstore."

"I recall your husband mentioning you had descended for a newspaper, Madame. But were you not also in the arcade for a considerable period of time?"

"Not really. I bought the paper, glanced through it in the lobby, and then returned to the arcade to browse some myself. As Mr. Randolph said, there is not really much else to do since we're being kept in the hotel like prisoners."

"Well, you know where I was," Grant Powell said. "As you recall, I was taking a shower when you arrived at our room."

"Perhaps you had just returned from the fifth floor," DeBevre said. "Perhaps you had just returned from committing murder."

Powell's face darkened with anger. "That's damned nonsense, and you know it!"

"Of course it is," Laura Powell said. "Grant couldn't have killed Tony Sprague or Ray Balfour or anyone else; he's not your murderer, Prefect."

"This may well be true," DeBevre observed darkly; "and then it may not be true at all. M'sieur Sprague's dying declaration might well point to your husband, Madame."

"What's that?" Mountbatten broke in. "Sprague was alive when you found him?"

"For only a moment, yes. But he lived long enough to utter one word, and that word was 'checkmate.'"

More murmurs of surprise rustled among the seven gathered suspects. Powell said, "All right, I see how that might point to me, in an indirect way. As everyone here knows, checkmate is a chess term meaning the king is dead. I don't suppose Sprague was referring to himself, but he might have been referring to me, as the probable new king of Transcon chess. However, he damned well wasn't."

Powell smiled thinly. "Then again, he might have been referring to Mountbatten, who is the current king of Transcon chess."

The British champion sat up in his chair, his own face reddening with outrage. "Rubbish!" he snapped. He glared at Powell and then looked at DeBevre. "If I had killed Sprague, why wouldn't he simply have spoken my name? Why take such a preposterously roundabout way of accusing someone?"

"But he did not speak the name of anyone," DeBevre reminded him. "He spoke the word 'checkmate.' There is no way to understand the workings of a dying man's fevered mind."

The Prefect turned his attention now to the dour, reticent features of Hans Dorner. The Swiss official was leaning against one wall, holding a cup of coffee in his hands, both of which trembled badly.

"Ah, Herr Dorner," DeBevre commented, "is that the effect of a hangover which is so obvious to all present? Or, perhaps, the outward sign of a guilty conscience?"

Dorner said thickly, "My conscience is as clear as yours. If I had known how I would feel this morning, I would never have entertained the idea of a drink to calm my nerves last night. One led to another, and I believe I had a schnapps for every year of my life."

DeBevre turned back to Clive Kettridge. But before he could resume his interrogation, there was a polite knock on the closed salon door. Then the door opened and the portly figure of Charlie Chan stepped inside.

"Please excuse my interruption," Chan said, "but it is necessary to request your most urgent assistance, Claude."

DeBevre hurried over to Chan. "What is it, Charlie?"

Chan's features betraying no sign of emotion, he said, "I believe probable identity of the murderer of Mr. Balfour and Mr. Sprague is in our possession."

The announcement was so calmly given that it was a moment before the others in the salon reacted. Then there was a series of surprised murmurs and exchanges of guarded looks, as everyone fastened their attention on the Honolulu detective.

"One of us?" Melvin Randolph asked. "You mean, one of us *here*?"

Chan said nothing. Prefect DeBevre's eyes were wide, and he asked with rising excitement, "Who is it, Charlie? How did you discover—?"

"I will offer a full explanation at a later time," Chan said. "First we are in need of absolute proof, for without it, our case is based on speculation only. As a house which has been built without a foundation, it would thus be in danger of collapse."

"What kind of proof, and how do we obtain it?"

"By a methodical search of the hotel," Charlie Chan told him. "The emphasis is to be placed on all the vacant rooms on the fourth, fifth, and sixth floors."

DeBevre was at a complete loss to understand. "But why vacant rooms?"

"If a clever murderer wishes to hide incriminating evidence, what more sensible place than one which seems senseless?"

Claude DeBevre said with full trust in Chan's capabilities, "As you wish, Charlie. I have little doubt that you, if not I, know of what you speak."

Chan nodded, then glanced at each of the seven suspects. None of their faces revealed any sign of guilt or apprehension, but Chan knew that one of them was a cold-blooded and extremely clever killer.

He said, "I suggest that all of you either remain here or return to your individual rooms while our search is being conducted. No one is to attempt to leave the hotel."

"Damn it all," Kettridge protested, "you should not make an announcement like the one you just made and then leave us in bloody suspense! The murderer must be desperate now that you've said you know his identity. He might kill more of us!"

"The possibility of any further deaths is remote," Charlie Chan said. "Please, remain calm and do not fear."

"That's easy for you to say," Randolph snapped. "Well, I for one am going to my room and lock the door and keep it locked until this business is finished once and for all."

"I shall do the same," Mountbatten concurred.

The others voiced similar sentiments, and Chan said to DeBevre, "Time, I fear, is a vital factor—now, more than ever. We must hurry."

"Oui, certainement!" DeBevre agreed, and the two detectives hastily left the salon.

The others shifted uneasily in their places, casting surreptitious looks at one another. Then, singularly and in pairs, they stood and began to file out.

XIV

CHARLIE CHAN made certain that the corridor was deserted before inserting the concierge's master key into the lock on the door marked 616. Opening the door and switching on the overhead chandelier, he and DeBevre slipped inside and Chan relocked the latch.

The Prefect's forehead was furrowed. "Why have we come here, Charlie? You said a search of the hotel was to be conducted."

"A search is no longer necessary," Chan told him. "Take a look at the chandelier above you."

"The chandelier?" DeBevre's frown deepened as he stared at the fixture. "It is the same as all others in the hotel."

"Not quite true." The portly detective moved an easy chair beneath the chandelier, stood on it, and stretched one hand up among its gilt vines and arms. It was only then that the Prefect was able to discern another object attached to one of the limbs. It was fastened by gilt-painted clamps, nearly invisible from a few feet away, camouflaged by more gold paint and the Baroque confusion of the chandelier's construction.

When Charlie Chan had finished undoing the contraption, he stepped down again and handed it to DeBevre.

"This," he said, "is the weapon which killed Raymond Balfour."

"Mon Dieu!"

The object which Claude DeBevre held was a short length of plumber's pipe, capped at one end, the other end open and slightly blackened from the discharge of the ball-bearing "bullet." Protruding through a hole in the end cap were two wires, which were connected to a small metal box some six inches square and three inches high. From the other side of the box was a strip of painted lamp-cord, its ends screwed to alligator clips the kind with a single pointed tip used for penetrating insulation.

"I believe," Chan said, "that the American term for this type of weapon is a 'zip gun.' Juvenile gangs often fashion similar guns in cities where real pistols are difficult to obtain."

"Ah, *mais oui!"* DeBevre exclaimed. "We find such guns as you describe among the Apaches of our Montmarte district. But this box, Charlie, and the wires . . . How are they included?"

"The box is a burglar alarm relay," Chan explained. "Normally, an alarm system is triggered when a weak electrical current is cut off, but there is also the opposite type which triggers the alarm when the current is on. These are used to confuse burglars who cut house wires and thus feel safe, for then an independent electrical current inside switches the relay and an alarm is rung."

"And this is the second type," DeBevre concluded. "But how was it used to fire the bearing?"

"The alligator clips punctured the electrical wires of the chandelier, and as long as the light was on, the relay remained open. But when Raymond Balfour, lying in bed, reached up and turned the light off at the switch over the headboard, the relay closed and the batteries inside fed a miniature transformer. The transformer, in turn, supplied enough spark to detonate the powder placed in the pipe barrel with the ball bearing."

"Powder," DeBevre echoed; and then with his eyes widening, he said, "Powder from the bullets in M'sieur Kettridge's revolver! *Alors!* I see it all now!"

"Yes. Then the empty cartridges were returned to the Webley," Charlie Chan amplified, "for the simple reason that there was nowhere else to dispose of them without fear of discovery."

The Prefect stared at Charlie Chan incredulously. "An ingenious method of murder. How did you discover it?"

"While lying in bed this morning, my eyes rested on the chandelier, and I became acutely aware of it. The chandelier in my room is the same as the one in the murder room and all other rooms in the hotel. It occurred to me that it would be a most excellent hiding place, overlooked by all last night. I obtained a passkey and proceeded to examine the murder room. On the floor beneath the fixture were particles of gilt paint. They obviously had fallen since the murder, for your technicians would otherwise have vacuumed them up.

"A further examination of the chandelier disclosed exposed electrical wiring to which the relay had been attached, and marks on the surface of one arm where the zip gun had been clamped."

"But once it had been removed," DeBevre said, "how did you deduce it would be here, in a vacant chamber?"

"By asking myself the question: where is the most logical hiding place, considering the hotel is secured? Obviously another chandelier. However, the murderer would not wish to be captured while in an occupied room, hence the choice of one that was vacant. While you were in the salon with the suspects, I searched all possible vacancies and discovered the weapon here, in room 616. It was as simple as that."

DeBevre's eyes were filled with respect. "It is to be devoutly wished that Claude DeBevre shall one day possess one-half the deductive logic of his friend, Charlie Chan." He paused with grim excitement. "And now, who is the killer? What is the name of the person who created this evil contrivance?"

"While my deductions have narrowed the choice to two, I am as yet unsure which one is guilty."

"But in the salon, you said you knew!"

"Forgive me, but it was done to deceive—not you, but the guilty party." Chan moved the chair back to where it had been. "I am hopeful that the killer will not guess that we already know in which room the weapon is hidden, and believe that we are busy elsewhere."

"Ah, and so he will come here to remove the weapon!"

"Yes," Chan replied. He gestured to the bathroom and smiled at the Prefect. "If you will be so kind as to turn off the chandelier, we will hide in here and see if my trap will ensnare the murderer. Only then will there be sufficient evidence to convict."

Chan and Prefect DeBevre entered the bathroom, keeping the door slightly ajar and all the lights out. The seconds ticked away into long, drawn-out minutes; finally, in a burst of impatience, the French detective whispered:

"You said there were only two suspects now, Charlie. Who are they? My curiosity, it is—"

Chan placed a warning finger to his lips. "I believe someone is now at the door."

Silence, except for the distant hum of an electric razor, was absolute. Then came the sound of a key inserted into the door, the turning of the latch, and footsteps in a quiet hurry.

Then a rustle as someone clicked on the chandelier and dragged a chair beneath it. Chan waited only for a second, then opening the door he said:

"The weapon is no longer hidden where you put it; it is now in the possession of the police."

The killer gasped,whirling and stumbling from the chair. Charlie Chan and Prefect DeBevre stood framed in the now open door to the bathroom, and the killer realized all at once that a trap had been set and that now it was sprung.

"Do not attempt to flee," DeBevre said. "There is no place for you to run."

Laura Powell stared at the two stern-faced detectives for a long moment. Then, bitterly accepting the fact that she had, after all, been placed in checkmate—that the game was indeed over—she sat on the chair, covered her face with her hands, and began to weep.

XV

CHARLIE CHAN felt little sympathy for the crying woman. He knew from his years of experience with crime and criminals that underneath her pretty facade she was calculating and ruthless, lacking a fundamental decency; her histrionics were hollow and more the result of self-pity than any sort of repentance.

Turning to DeBevre, the Oriental detective said sorrowfully, "When hatred gains control of a woman, that which is man's greatest joy becomes his deadliest enemy."

"All too true, Charlie." DeBevre's lips were compressed tightly. "It is apparent to me now that your other suspect was Madame Powell's husband, Grant Powell. Is this not so, my friend?"

"Yes. I arrived at that conclusion due to the Powell's sudden exchange of rooms with Mr.

Balfour."

DeBevre frowned. "But would not the exchange allow for the Powells to be the intended victims as well as M'sieur Balfour?"

"On the surface, perhaps," Chan answered. "Yet consider: the room has but one bed, a double bed in which the Powells would sleep together. One shot was fired into the center of the bed, where only a man who was alone would be lying. Hence, it is reasonable to assume the killer wished only to dispose of a single man, and since the Powells and Mr. Balfour told no one else of the room switch, the choice was thus narrowed to only one of two people as the probable murderer."

"Ah, I understand," DeBevre said. "I did not think of that, poor Prefect that I am." He looked at Laura Powell. "Now, then, Madame. Why did you murder M'sieur Balfour?"

"Love," she sobbed bitterly. "Love . . . and hate!"

"The opposites which are inseparable?" Chan said. "I recall the conversation with Jennifer Kettridge in which she stated she did not care for Mr. Balfour's treatment of women. I also remember Tony Sprague's comment last night concerning Mr. Balfour's behavior with married ladies. Could it be, Mrs. Powell, that you and Mr. Balfour were having an affair?"

"Yes," she answered, "for a number of years. I loved him, far more than I ever loved Grant." A shudder passed through her. "But Ray grew tired of me, laughed at me when I refused to break it off so he could have that young Kettridge girl. Oh, I know she resisted his advances, but Ray was very clever and he would have won her over after a while. If not, then it would have been some other girl."

Her eyes, puffed and red from crying, now flashed with dark rage. "And when he threatened to tell all to Grant and that reporter, Sprague, drag my good name through the mud . . . well, it was then I knew I had to make sure he never left me. I tried to kill him up on the roof terrace, after insisting on a showdown meeting, but Kettridge's faulty pistol failed to fire. If I had checked it more carefully, none of this would have happened."

"How did you know of M'sieur Kettridge's gun?"

"Ray told me. Jennifer, in resisting him, had threatened that her father would use it if he didn't leave her alone. Instead, it was I who used it."

"You stole the gun from Mr. Kettridge's room?" Chan asked.

"Yes. The hotel staff is very careful with the keys, but I bided my time and finally was able briefly to steal the custodian's set. I took the passkey immediately to have a duplicate made. Then I replaced the original and waited for a chance to take the gun."

"This duplicate was also used to enter the murder room so you could remove the weapon last night," Chan said, "as well as to enter this room and the one in which Tony Sprague died."

"Yes."

DeBevre asked, "How is it, Madame, that you knew enough to make such a device as the one you used to kill M'sieur Balfour?"

"I lived in Brooklyn as a child," she said, her head lowered. "My brother ran with a gang. He used zip guns. And then, before I married Grant, I was a secretary in an engineering firm. I've always had an aptitude for things mechanical—though now I wish I never had."

"Go on," Chan said.

Laura Powell moaned slightly with self-pity. "Once I hit upon the idea, I spent most of yesterday buying and having the different parts made, being careful to do it in various parts of Paris so none could be traced to me. Then I built it and painted it, and installed it in the chandelier while Grant was elsewhere. All I had to do then was to convince Grant to switch rooms with Ray, to make it seem as if Grant were the intended victim and that way, deepen the mystery."

Chan asked quietly, "You murdered Tony Sprague because he learned you had done away with Mr. Balfour?"

"Indirectly. I removed the zip gun from Ray's room around four this morning, using the duplicate key, and Sprague happened to be awake, unable to sleep. He must have heard me—his room was right across the hall from ours, as you recall—and he saw me leaving. He followed me when I went down for the paper after breakfast, which was when I thought of how to hide the zip gun in a vacant room."

"And he walked in on you while you were hiding it in the vacant chamber on the fifth floor."

"Yes. The maid was working on the room when I came by and I could tell as I passed that it was a vacant one. So after she'd moved on, I let myself in. I was fastening the zip gun to the chandelier when Sprague walked in. He took one look at the weapon and knew I'd killed Ray, knew it for certain. He said he was going to turn me in and take credit for solving the murder."

"Will you explain about Mr. Kettridge's gun, please?"

"I had it with me. I was going to hide it in the room as well—inside the toilet tank, someplace like that where no guests or maids ever look. Sprague jumped me and took the Webley away without knowing it was faulty. I saw the knife by the bowl of fruit and in desperation I . . . I picked it up and stabbed him. I didn't know what to do next.

"I couldn't leave the zip gun in the chandelier in that room for the same reason I couldn't leave it in Ray's room: you might eventually discover it with a more careful search. So I took it down again, but left the pistol in Sprague's hand; I thought it would confuse things further. It probably wasn't a good idea, but Sprague was still alive and moaning on the floor, and I . . . I wasn't thinking clearly."

"Then you went to the sixth floor and found a similar vacancy—this room—in which to hide the zip gun."

Laura Powell nodded.

DeBevre said, "There is but one detail which bothers me," he said to Chan. "I understand how Madame Powell killed two men, and why, and how you deduced the significance of the vacant rooms. But I cannot fathom M'sieur Sprague's dying declaration."

"The ways of a dying man's mind are impossible to understand," Chan said, "but it seems certain that he was attempting in a roundabout fashion to name his murderer. Checkmate is a single word when used in the game of chess, but it is also a combination of two separate words: check and mate.

"Mr. Sprague, then, wanted us to 'check mate', and the only married couple in this case is the Powells. When a man refers to a mate, it is usually to the female partner, and so I suspected that the guilty party was indeed Mrs. Powell. Unfortunately, I could not prove it without this ruse."

"You are truly amazing," DeBevre said with admiration. "And now at last the game is over, the queen has fallen, and checkmate has been achieved; the analogy to chess is a strong one indeed. But without you, there would have been a different end to this match of wits."

"Perhaps," Chan said self-effacingly. "But in the contest of murder, the criminal seldom makes all the proper moves and eventually is defeated by trapping himself."

As DeBevre went to the room's telephone to call the Prefecture, Laura Powell put her face in her hands again and began once more to weep.

XVI

CHARLIE CHAN stood beside the expansive lobby desk, watching one of the porters bring his worn brown leather suitcase from the elevator. DeBevre, once again polishing his glasses, stood next to the Honolulu detective and sadly reflected, "Ah, my good friend, these past three weeks of your vacation in Paris have flown by too swiftly. Must you return?"

"Alas, the choice is not mine," Chan said with a warm smile. "But I shall return to your city soon, I promise."

Grant Powell, accompanied by Clive and Jennifer Kettridge, entered the lobby from the arcade and hurried across to say good-bye to Charlie Chan. After amenities, Chan said to the American chess expert, "I enjoyed greatly the playing of your fifth game yesterday. A most challenging new gambit."

"Thank you, Mr. Chan."

"It was quite a game," Kettridge agreed. "Powell's now a point ahead of Roger—a close tournament."

"And a fair one," Jennifer said, "as it was from the start."

Kettridge said ruefully and with uncustomary self-deprecation, "Yes, quite so. We were all extremely bullheaded at the beginning of the Transcon tournament, and it took a tragedy such as we all experienced to make us realize it. That is the only genuinely happy thing to come out of the horror of three weeks ago."

A shadow fell across Grant Powell's handsome features. "The shock of learning that my wife was a murderess was immense at first. I had suspected for some time that she was having an affair, but I had no idea it was with Ray Balfour. I knew, too, that our marriage was about over—there was no love left between us. But it was still a terrible shock, and one which brought home to me what a child I've been about so many things, what a naive and arrogant fool I've been."

Powell sighed. "Still, with all those reporters and their endless questions, and the way the case was played up in the news media . . . well, I wanted nothing except to leave Paris and go into hiding somewhere, alone with my shame. I wanted nothing more to do with the chess tournament. But then Mr.

Chan pointed out to me that running away would solve nothing, that if I fled this crisis I would never be able to face myself again; and that if I was truly a changed man, I would continue with the tournament."

Chan inclined his head.

"He was right," Powell contined, "as I've found Mr. Chan usually is. I now still have my self-respect, and Transcon chess has managed to survive all the adverse publicity—particularly since Roger Mountbatten and Kettridge here and I have patched up our differences and begun to act like gentlemen."

DeBevre's and Chan's eyes contained a newfound respect for the young American chess expert. And in Jennifer Kettridge's eyes, there was open admiration. To Chan at least, it was quite obvious that if she had her way, Grant Powell would find a lasting love with her, a love that would be strong rather than destructive.

"I believe we all owe Mr. Chan a great debt," Kettridge said. "He has done us a vast good service."

"I am pleased to have been of some small assistance," Charlie Chan said slowly. "But I cannot take credit for individual perceptions. Wisdom is purchased by one's own experience and understanding, and this is what makes a man fit company for himself and for others."

DeBevre said, "Charlie, you are not only a great detective but a great philosopher as well!"

Chan bowed as his taxi was announced. "Detection and philosophy are one and the same," he said. "Both are the sad consideration of human folly."

THE END

Printed in the United States
88274LV00005B/160/A